Still a Family

BRENDA REEVES STURGIS

pictures by
JO-SHIN LEE

Albert Whitman & Company
Chicago, Illinois

We live in the city shelter.
My mom, my doll, and me.

My dad lives in a different shelter, down another street.
But we are still a family.

I sleep on a cot near my mom.
Bunk beds border the walls in a large room.

People snore.
Subways roar.
Buses, cars, and taxis honk.
I toss and turn and try to fall asleep.

I miss my quiet room,
my comfy bed, and my
cozy quilt.

I cuddle with my doll, Molly.
And even though my dad isn't here
to tuck me in, we are still a family.

While the older kids are at school, I play.
Cots make fun forts!
Sometimes…I don't want to come out from under the bed.

I share my doll with the girl beside me.
We take turns all afternoon.
My new friend calls Molly "Madeline."
I think it's okay if my doll has two names.

Some days we meet my dad at the park.
We slide on slides.
Hide-and-seek is our most favorite game of all.

Sometimes we stop to pet puppies or sniff the flowers.
We are together, and we are still a family.

"I love you to the moon and back," Dad says.
"I love you to the moon and back two times," I reply.

Dad blows us a kiss. We catch it in the air QUICK!
My mom, my doll, and me.

We blow kisses back and forth until we are out of sight.
And even though Dad goes one way and we go another, we are still a family.

One rainy day we fish a tattered tarp out of a trash can,
and we make a lean-to.

My head gets wet,
but I don't care.
Mom finger combs
my hair and then
braids it.

Dad hugs us both tight in that small squished space.
We are together, and we are still a family.

My parents look for work every day
and take turns taking care of me.

We scrimp and save all our pennies.
And even though my shoes are a little snug, I don't complain too much.

We stand in long lines that snake around the corner.

Waiting such a long time to eat is hard, but I try my best to smile.

And even though my belly grumbles,
I share my food with my doll.
    She likes the beef stew best of all.

Days and weeks and months go by.

We celebrate holidays.

And even though we live in different shelters,
we are still a family.

On my birthday, Dad lights a candle on my chocolate cupcake.
"Make a wish," my mom says.
I close my eyes tight.

Then I blow out the candle,
share my cupcake with my doll,
and smile.

Because we are STILL a family!

Author's Note

In practically every city homeless people can be found. Sometimes a few paychecks are all that separate those who have a home from those who live in a shelter. People can live in shelters from a few days to over a year, and some people live in shelters for several years. This book was conceived after an online discussion about how to explain homelessness to children. I broached this story thoughtfully and carefully to raise awareness and give the children who live in shelters a voice. I wanted to tell this story through the eyes of a child and what she may hope for when her family is separated by dire circumstances. There are thousands of shelters across the country but very few where families can stay intact. It is difficult enough for a child to live in a shelter, and being separated from family members because of necessity creates another level of stress. If you are a child living in a homeless shelter, I want you to know that you are not alone. People care, and this book was written for you.

I hope this book touches a million hearts, and I hope those hearts are stirred to take a stand and make a difference. There are many ways we can all help. Consider donating items that people in shelters need, such as socks or shoes, or giving money to assist the homeless with getting birth certificates, state ID cards, and subway or bus passes to travel to job interviews. Another way to assist is by serving in a soup kitchen or starting a fund-raiser. The needs of the homeless are limitless. Whatever you can do will matter, and it will help.

Resources

National Alliance to End Homelessness
www.endhomelessness.org

National Coalition for the Homeless
nationalhomeless.org

Coalition for the Homeless
www.coalitionforhomeless.org

StandUp for Kids
www.standupforkids.org

Family Promise
www.familypromise.org

National Center on Family Homelessness
www.air.org

Acknowledgments

I am thankful to the team at Albert Whitman, especially to my editor, Andrea Hall, for their belief in me and in this story. And with greatest love and appreciation to my agent and friend, Karen Grencik, and to Tracey Adams for the inspiration.

To all the families and children that live, or have lived,
in a homeless shelter and to anybody that can make a difference—BRS

To dear Peishin, thank you for all your support—JL

Library of Congress Cataloging-in-Publication data is on file with the publisher.

Text copyright © 2017 by Brenda Reeves Sturgis
Pictures copyright © 2017 by Albert Whitman & Company
Pictures by Jo-Shin Lee
Published in 2017 by Albert Whitman & Company
ISBN 978-0-8075-7707-3
Printed in China
10 9 8 7 6 5 4 3 2 1 HH 20 19 18 17 16

Design by Jordan Kost

For more information about Albert Whitman & Company,
visit our web site at www.albertwhitman.com.